THIS IS A BORZOI BOOK PUBLISHED BY ALFRED A. KNOPF

Copyright © 2002, 2003 by Hachette Livre

www.randomhouse.com/kids

Library of Congress Cataloging-in-Publication Data:
Gutman, Anne.
[Lisa dans la jungle. English]
Lisa in the jungle / Anne Gutman, Georg Hallensleben.—1st ed.
p. cm.
(The misadventures of Gaspard and Lisa)
Summary: Although she spent the summer at the community swimming pool, Lisa tells her
classmates that she visited the jungle where her uncle raises panthers and leopards.
ISBN 0-375-82254-2
[1. Honesty—Fiction. 2. Jungles—Fiction. 3. Schools—Fiction. 4. Tall tales.]
I. Hallensleben, Georg. II. Title. III. Series.
PZ7.G9844 Lj 2003
[E]—dc21   2002013200

PRINTED IN FRANCE by Pollina n° L88342
September 2003
10 9 8 7 6 5 4 3 2 1
First American Edition

ANNE GUTMAN · GEORG HALLENSLEBEN

Lisa in the Jungle

Alfred A. Knopf ✦ New York

This summer we didn't go on vacation. All I did was go swimming in the community pool every day. So on the first day of school, when Gaspard showed everyone photos of him sailing, I was really jealous.

"I went to the jungle," I said, "to visit my uncle who raises panthers and leopards." Everyone stopped talking . . .

and I told them the story of my fabulous vacation in the jungle.

Uncle Paul picked me up in his private plane.
We flew all day and all night before we
arrived at his place in the jungle.

Two gigantic gorillas guarded his house. They
niffed me and let me pass because they remembered
me—they had met me when I was a baby.

My uncle's house was high in a tree. On the trunk was a secret code to open the door.

I had a room all to myself. There was a big bed covered in ostrich feathers and on the nightstand a parrot named George.

In the morning, George woke me, squawking, "Lisa, rise and shine!"

There is no electricity in the jungle, so my uncle could not have a vacuum cleaner. Instead he had an anteater.

The anteater was very good at cleaning up the crumbs from breakfast.

After breakfast, my uncle wanted to show me his land. We started off by riding on elephants.

To get to the panthers, we had to cross a river full of crocodiles and then a lake of man-eating piranha fish. At the river we waited until the crocodiles were all napping, and then . . .

. . . we quietly climbed onto the back of one of them and drifted to the other side of the river.

To cross the lake filled with hungry piranhas, Uncle Paul had a chairlift that took us high above the water.

Finally we came to the preserve
with 100 black panthers and spotted
leopards. We fed them and then, one
by one, gave each a good brushing.
They purred loudly.

There was a tiny baby leopard that I fed with
a bottle every day. He thought I was his mother
and followed me everywhere!

When I started telling how I clipped the claws of
this little baby leopard, our teacher appeared.
She said it was time for us to return to class.

In the classroom, Pierre turned around and asked me if I had brought my baby leopard home. I was going to say yes when he said that my story was very strange and if I had really been in the jungle . . .

. . . why had he seen me in the community
swimming pool all summer long?
OH, NO!
What could I say?

Luckily, our teacher said, "That's enough, Pierre."

And Pierre was scolded for talking in class.

As for me, I will go to the zoo on Saturday and take photos to prove that I really was in the jungle!